$\mathcal{L}$ittle
Red Riding Hood

BY

The Brothers Grimm

Retold by Jennifer Greenway

ILLUSTRATED BY

Elizabeth Miles

ARIEL BOOKS

ANDREWS AND McMEEL
KANSAS CITY

Library of Congress Cataloging-in-Publication Data

Eisen, Armand.
    Little Red Riding Hood / the Brothers Grimm ; illustrated by
Elizabeth Miles.
        p.   cm.
    "Ariel books."
    Summary: A little girl meets a hungry wolf in the forest while on
her way to visit her grandmother.
    ISBN 0-8362-4901-1 : $6.95
    [1. Fairy tales. 2. Folklore—Germany.] I. Grimm, Wilhelm,
1786-1859. II. Grimm, Jacob, 1785-1863. III. Miles, Elizabeth J.,
ill. IV. Little Red Riding Hood. English. V. Title.
PZ8.E36Li   1992
398.2—dc20
[E]   91-33982
                                                          CIP
                                                           AC

Design: Susan Hood and Mike Hortens
Art Direction: Armand Eisen, Mike Hortens, and Julie Phillips
Art Production: Lynn Wine
Production: Julie Miller and Lisa Shadid

Little
Red Riding Hood

$\mathcal{T}$here once lived a girl whose name was Little Red Riding Hood. She was called that because she always wore a red velvet cloak and hood that her grandmother had made for her.

Now her grandmother had been feeling ill, and one day Little Red Riding Hood's mother said to her, "I want you to take this basket of cakes and honey to Granny."

"Now go straight to Granny's," her mother told her, "and be sure you don't speak to any strangers on the way, and whatever you do, don't stray from the path!" Little Red Riding Hood promised to do as she was told.

Her grandmother lived on the other side of a great forest. So, Little Red Riding Hood went skipping quickly down the path with her basket under her arm.

She had not gone far when she met a big wolf.

"Good morning, Little Red Riding Hood," said the wolf. "Where are you going in such a hurry?"

Little Red Riding Hood did not know what a wicked creature the wolf was, so she replied politely, "I am going to see my grandmother. She has been ill, and I am bringing her this basket of cakes and honey."

"How nice," said the wolf. But to himself he thought, "What good luck! If I am clever I can have both Little Red Riding Hood and her grandmother for supper!"

Then he smiled at Little Red Riding Hood and said, "How lovely the woods look today! What a pity you have to rush on such a beautiful morning!"

Little Red Riding Hood looked around. Sunbeams were dancing in the trees, and bright flowers were waving their heads in the breeze. "I'm sure Grandmother would love a bouquet of flowers," she thought. "It's so early that surely I can stop for just a few minutes and pick some."

So Little Red Riding Hood left the path and skipped into the woods to pick flowers. Meanwhile the wolf ran as fast as he could to Grandmother's house.

When the wolf reached Grandmother's house, he knocked on the door.

"Who's there?" called Little Red Riding Hood's grandmother.

"It is I, Little Red Riding Hood!" said the wolf, disguising his voice. "I've brought you a basket of cakes and honey."

"I am too sick to get out of bed," Grandmother replied. "But the door is open, Little Red Riding Hood, just let yourself in and come up to my bedroom."

So the wicked wolf pushed open the door, came inside, and climbed the stairs to Grandmother's bedroom. Then he went to Grandmother's bed and gobbled up the old woman!

Then the wicked wolf pulled one of Grandmother's flannel nightgowns over his head, even though it was much too small for him. Next, he put on Grandmother's warm woolen dressing gown. He even took Grandmother's spectacles and stuck them on the end of his long nose.

Then the wolf looked at himself in the mirror. He didn't look anything like Grandmother. And his long ears were showing. So the wolf put on Grandmother's lace nightcap, to try to hide them.

Then he climbed into Grandmother's bed, drew the covers over his nose, and settled back to wait for Little Red Riding Hood.

Meanwhile Little Red Riding Hood was still in the woods picking flowers. Every time she picked one, she seemed to see a prettier one just a little ways off. And so she strayed farther and farther from the path.

When she had picked so many flowers that she could not hold even one more, she returned to the path and headed again for Grandmother's house.

When Little Red Riding Hood arrived, she was surprised to find the door open.

"Hello," she called. "Grandmother, it's me."

"Just come in!" came Grandmother's voice. "I am too ill to get out of bed!"

How strange her grandmother's voice sounded. "She must be very ill," thought Little Red Riding Hood. So the little girl ran up the stairs to her grandmother's bedroom.

Little Red Riding Hood stood beside her grandmother's bed. How strange her grandmother looked!

"Why, Grandmother," she said. "What big ears you have!"

"All the better to hear you with, my dear," said the wolf.

"But, Grandmother, what big eyes you have!" said Little Red Riding Hood.

"All the better to see you with, my dear," said the wolf.

"But, Grandmother, what big hands you have!" said Little Red Riding Hood.

"All the better to hug you with, my dear," said the wolf.

"But, Grandmother," said Little Red Riding Hood. "What big teeth you have!"

"All the better to eat you with, my dear," said the wolf.

And with that the wicked wolf jumped out of the bed and opened his jaws wide.

"Why, you're not Grandmother!" cried Little Red Riding Hood.

"No, I'm not," said the wolf. "And I'm going to eat you up!"

Then the wolf snapped at Little Red Riding Hood and swallowed her in a single gulp!

After that, the wolf felt full. He rubbed his belly contentedly. "That was a good meal," he said, and then he started to yawn. "Now I could do with a nap!"

So the wolf climbed back into Grandmother's bed. Then he pulled the covers over his head and closed his eyes.

Soon the wolf was fast asleep and he began to snore very loudly. He snored so loudly that all the windows in Grandmother's house rattled.

Toward evening, a huntsman came walking by and heard the wolf snoring.

"That is strange," he thought to himself. "The old woman is snoring awfully loudly! I wonder if she is all right."

So the huntsman walked up to Grandmother's house. To his great surprise the door was wide open. "Hello! Hello!" called the huntsman. "Is anybody home?"

But there was no answer. The wicked wolf was sleeping too soundly to hear the huntsman.

"I'll just go in and make sure everything is all right," the huntsman thought. So he went inside and tiptoed up the stairs.

As he climbed the stairs, the snoring grew louder and louder. The huntsman followed the snoring all the way to Grandmother's bed.

The huntsman looked at Grandmother's bed and saw the wolf lying fast asleep.

"Ah-ha," said the huntsman. "So it's you who is snoring so loudly, you rascal! I've been hunting for you for a long time, and now it looks as if I've got you!"

The huntsman raised his gun and was about to shoot the wolf when it occurred to him that the wolf might have eaten the old woman.

So the huntsman took a knife and cut open the wolf. Out stepped Little Red Riding Hood and her grandmother. They were both happy to be saved.

Then the huntsman filled the wolf's stomach with heavy stones and sewed it up. When the wolf awoke and saw the huntsman, he tried to run away. But the stones were so heavy that he fell down dead!

Then the huntsman, Little Red Riding Hood, and Grandmother ate all the delicious cakes and honey that Little Red Riding Hood had brought.

Soon Grandmother was feeling well again, and Little Riding Hood started home.

When she returned, Little Red Riding Hood told her mother everything that had happened. "Never again will I speak to strangers or stray from the path when you have told me not to!" she said.

Her mother hugged her tight. "I'm sure you won't," she said, and Little Red Riding Hood never did!